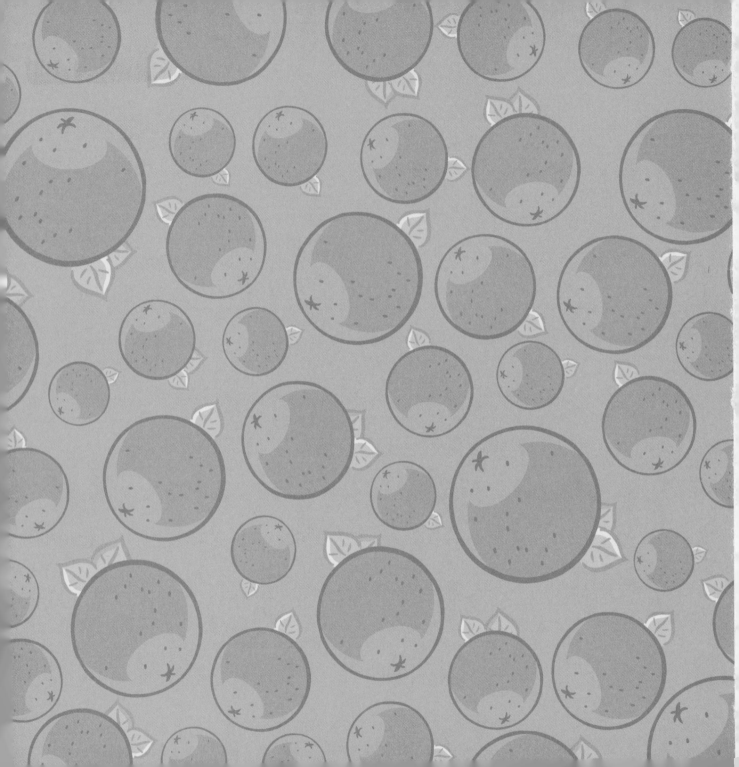

Strawberry Shortcake™ Crafts Club

ORANGE BLOSSOM'S FRUITY FUN BOOK

A Juicy Orange Adventure

by Nicole Okaty

Scholastic Inc.

New York   Toronto   London   Auckland   Sydney   Mexico City   New Delhi   Hong Kong   Buenos Aires

ISBN 0-439-70466-9

Designer: Emily Muschinske
Illustrations: Lisa and Terry Workman
Photographs: Nicole Okaty

12 11 10 9 8 7 6 5 4 3 2 1   4 5 6 7 8 9/0

Printed in the U.S.A.
First Scholastic printing, December 2004

TABLE OF CONTENTS

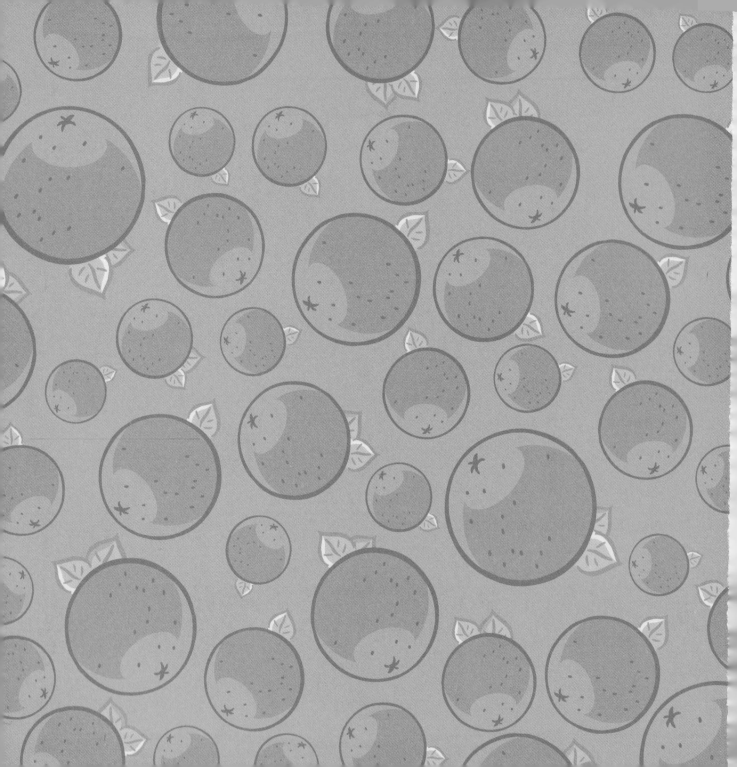

Get Ready for an
ALL-ORANGE ADVENTURE!

Welcome to Orange Blossom Acres! I live here, inside a special tree house, with my pet butterfly, Marmalade. We make the berry best juice, using fruits from the trees in my orchard. I love everything orange—and I like to dress in orange clothes, too.

Orange Blossom and I will be making orange crafts, playing orange games, and mixing up some berrylicious orange recipes. Orange you glad we're going to have so much fun together?

We'll have a frutti tutti time! So grab your Orange Craft Kit and let's get going!

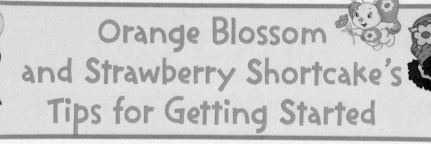

Orange Blossom and Strawberry Shortcake's Tips for Getting Started

1. Set up a space of your berry own where you can create your orange activities! If needed, cover your work space with newspaper to keep it clean.

2. Read the step by steps and collect the materials you'll need before starting a new project.

3. Whenever you see this picture throughout the book, it means that you can find what you need in your craft kit.

4. Some of the materials you'll need can be found around your house. You can get other materials at your grocery or craft store.

5. Put on an apron or an art smock before starting a project that could get messy—like when you mix food coloring in some of the recipes.

6. You may need a grown-up's help with some of the activities in the book. Whenever you see this symbol, you'll know to ask for help.

Berry Funny

Q: How many oranges grow on an orange tree?

A: All of them!

Getting Ready to Create with Oranges

Many of the recipes in this book use fresh oranges and other fruits. Here are a few tips:

1. When choosing oranges, look for ones that are firm and heavy for their size. That means the oranges are berry juicy!

2. Store your oranges in the refrigerator and use them within two weeks.

3. Wash the oranges in cold water before you peel them.

4. Always ask a grown-up to slice oranges (or any other fruits), if the recipe needs it.

Getting Ready to Use the Markers and Butterfly Stencil

1. Always put the caps back on your markers when you're finished, so the tips don't dry out.

2. Try not to use lighter colors on top of darker colors, or the tips of the lighter markers will become discolored.

3. Use a pencil to trace your stencil first. That way, you can erase any mistakes you make. Then fill in the shapes with markers.

4. Practice holding your butterfly stencil on the paper with one hand, while carefully tracing the shape with your other hand. Try not to wiggle or move the stencil.

Turn the page to visit Orange Blossom's tree house!

Juicy Marker Projects

Make Orange Blossom's tree house stand up and bloom with frutti tutti color and lots of stickers!

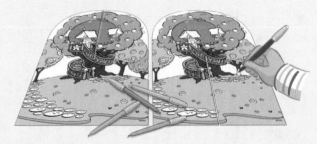

2. It's time to color! Use your marker set to color Orange Blossom's tree house. Color in the big orange, the big tree trunk, and the tree's leaves.

What You Need

- 2 cardboard tree house cut-outs
- Markers
- 2 sticker sheets (with 47 stickers)

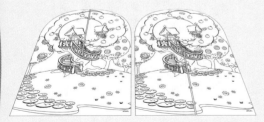

1. Lay the cardboard cut-outs flat on a table. There are 4 sides to color in all.

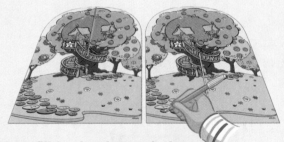

3. Now fill in the door, windows, and staircase on Orange Blossom's tree house with your markers. Color in the rest of the picture, any way you like.

6

4. To make your tree house stand up, line the slits up in each tree house piece, and slide them together, as shown.

5. Use your stickers to decorate your tree house. How will you decorate each side? Where will you put the Strawberry Shortcake and Orange Blossom stickers? You can put one Strawberry Shortcake and one Orange Blossom on each of the 4 sides of your tree.

Did you know that Orange Blossom is named after the flower that grows on an orange tree? And did you know that orange trees can have flowers, leaves, and fruit all at the same time? It's berry true!

6. Add oranges, flowers, and other stickers to your tree where you like. Display your Orange Blossom tree house as a sweet and fruity decoration!

What's round, orange, and polka dotted? Turn the page to see!

Polka Dot Orange

This juicy orange looks just like the ones that grow in Orange Blossom's orchard!

1. Turn your construction paper sideways. Using your pencil, draw a round orange shape with leaves onto your paper. Add flower shapes for orange blossoms, if you like.

What You Need

- 1 sheet of yellow or light-colored construction paper
- Pencil
- Markers (orange and green)
- White crayon

2. Take your orange marker and press the tip gently on the circle of your orange drawing. Lift it up to see a small dot. Repeat many times, to make many dots, to outline your orange shape.

3. Fill in your orange shape with your marker, making dots like you did in step 2.

4. Outline and fill in the leaves with dots using your green marker.

5. Outline your orange blossom flowers like you did in step 2. Add a round orange center to each, if you like. Color your flower petals with a white crayon.

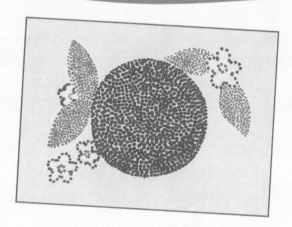

Berry Funny

Q: Why did the orange go to the doctor?

A: It wasn't "peeling" well!

Here's More: Now that you know how to make a dot drawing, you can make a bunch of oranges and more orange blossoms! How many oranges will you draw? Will you make them different sizes? It's up to you!

Turn the page for a dot drawing that's twice as sweet!

Orange Slices and Strawberries

Orange Blossom and I love to draw oranges and strawberries—can you guess why?

What You Need

- 1 sheet of light-colored construction paper
- Pencil
- Markers (orange, red, green, brown)

2. Draw 3 triangles inside each orange slice, as shown.

1. Turn your construction paper sideways. With your pencil, draw five half circles (orange slices) and five different-sized strawberries all over your paper.

3. With your orange marker, outline the half circles with dots like you did for Polka Dot Orange (on page 8).

4. Fill in the triangles inside your orange slices with orange dots.

5. Using the red marker, outline and fill in the strawberry shapes with dots. Use the brown marker to add dots for strawberry seeds.

Did you know that navel oranges are the most popular eating oranges in the world? They're seedless, easy to peel, and juicy, and they taste yummy!

Here's More: What other kinds of fruit can you draw by making lots of dots? Cherries? Apples? Blueberries?

6. Outline and fill in the leaves of the strawberries with green dots.

Turn the page to look for some of Marmalade's fluttering friends!

Butterfly Fun and Games

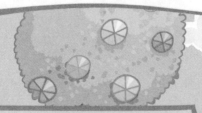

Butterfly Garden Hunt

Can you help Orange Blossom find Marmalade and five of her fluttering friends in this berry beautiful butterfly garden?

- I spy a pink butterfly with swirls on its wings and a green butterfly hidden in leaves.

- I spy Orange Blossom's friend, Marmalade, and a bright blue butterfly resting in the shade.

- I spy a yellow butterfly with stripes like a bee and a brown butterfly in a basket by a tree.

What else do you see?

- Can you find a little caterpillar crunching— and a white moth munching—on leaves?

(Turn to page 38 for the answers.)

3. Cut your butterflies out with scissors. Punch a hole at the top of each butterfly with a hole punch (or have an adult make a hole using a pencil).

6. Tie the butterfly on the shortest piece of yarn to the middle of the drinking straw. Tie the other two butterflies onto each end of the straw.

4. To make your mobile, cut 30 inches of yarn and thread it through the plastic drinking straw. Tie the ends of the yarn together with a knot.

5. Cut the rest of your yarn to make a short, a medium, and a long piece. Tie one butterfly to each piece of yarn, using the hole you made in step 3.

Here's More: Hang your mobile next to a window and watch your butterflies flutter in the breeze!

Turn the page to make a garden for your butterflies to flutter in!

Friendship Grows Like a Flower

Orange Blossom and I love to cut and paste this friendship flower garden together!

What You Need

- Construction paper (orange, pink, red, and yellow)
- Pencil
- Scissors
- White craft glue or school glue
- 4 craft sticks
- Green marker
- 1 cup salt
- Large sealable bag
- Food coloring (green and yellow)
- Small plastic container

2. Cut out the flower shape. Use the shape as a pattern to make three more flowers in different colors.

1. Using your pencil, draw a flower shape that measures about 2-x-2 inches onto a berry bright sheet of construction paper.

3. Using different colors of construction paper, cut out a round center for each of your flowers. Then glue the center inside each flower.

4. Color four craft sticks green, using your marker. Add a spot of glue to one end of each stick. Attach the blossoms to the sticks (flower stems). Let the glue dry.

7. Fill the plastic container with the green salt (grass). Push the craft sticks (your flower stems) into the grass and arrange the flowers in your garden.

5. You can create your own small blooming bouquet. To make nice spring green grass, pour the salt into a sealable bag. Add 15 drops of green food coloring and 10 drops of yellow food coloring.

6. Close the bag, rub in the food coloring, and shake it to make a nice shade of grass green.

Here's More: You can give your flowers to your berry best friend. Friendship grows (with love and care) like a flower!

Turn the page for a fruity and fun game!

Mix n' Match Fruit Game

It's fruit-picking time in Orange Blossom Acres and the trees look rather bare. Where are the fruits?

Did you know that fruits grow on trees, bushes, and vines? It's berry true!

1. oranges

2. bananas

3. strawberries

Match the fruits shown in each of Orange Blossom's baskets on this page to the trees and plants on the next page.

(Turn to page 38 for the answers.)

4. watermelons

5. blueberries

A. _____ patch

B. _____ vine

C. _____ bush

D. _____ tree

E. _____ tree

Mark your place in this fruity and fun book with the craft project on the next page!

23

Fruity Bookmarks

Orange Blossom and I love to read books with these juicy bookmarks!

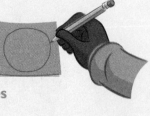

1. Using your pencil, draw a round orange shape that measures about 2-x-2-inches onto a sheet of orange construction paper.

What You Need

- Construction paper (in fruit colors like orange, green, purple, red, and also brown)
- Pencil
- Scissors
- Markers
- 4 craft sticks
- White craft glue or school glue

2. Cut out the orange with scissors.

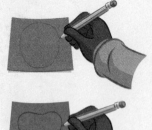

3. Repeat steps 1 and 2 three more times, to make different kinds of fruits, like strawberries, plums, and apples.

4. Use your markers and construction paper to add details, like fruit stems and seeds, on your fruit cut-outs.

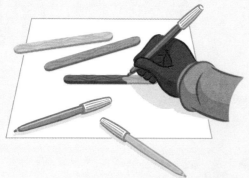

5. Color your craft sticks any shade you like, with your markers.

Here's More: What other fruits can you think of for more Fruity Bookmarks? It's up to you!

6. Add a spot of glue to one tip of each craft stick. Center the fruit and attach it to a stick. Let the glue dry.

Turn the page to find a bunch of juicy ways to count to ten!

5 Ways to Slice an Orange

*I*t's time for a juicy counting game! Look at the groups of orange slices on the next page. Can you pair each group with another group to make 10 slices all together?

Here's an example: If you have 6 orange slices, how many more slices do you need to get 10?

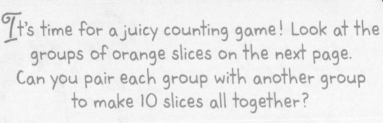

 +  = 10

Hint:

$$1 \smile + ? = 10 \smile$$
$$2 \smile + ? = 10 \smile$$
$$3 \smile + ? = 10 \smile$$
$$4 \smile + ? = 10 \smile$$
$$5 \smile + ? = 10 \smile$$

Berry Funny

Q: Why did the orange stop rolling down the hill?

A: It ran out of juice!

(Turn to page 38 for the answers.)

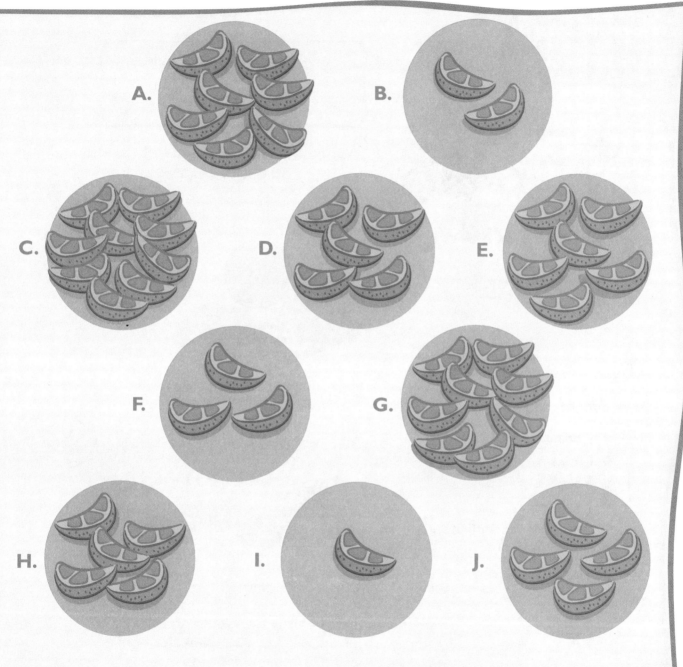

A.

B.

C.

D.

E.

F.

G.

H.

I.

J.

Turn the page for a real tutti frutti cutie!

Orange Blossom's Caterpillar

Orange Blossom and I love to make this colorful caterpillar!

1. Have an adult cut two oranges into round slices about $1/2$-inch thick.

What You Need

- 2 oranges
- Raisins
- 5 blueberries
- 1 strawberry
- Utensils: Knife, cutting board, large plate

Makes: 1 caterpillar

2. Arrange 4 large orange rounds on a plate—this will be your caterpillar's head and body. Add a smaller orange round at the end for the tail.

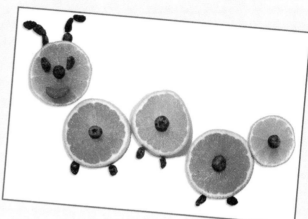

3. Make your caterpillar's face with two raisins for eyes, a blueberry for a nose, and a sliver of strawberry for a smile. Use more raisins to make two antennae on your caterpillar's head.

Here's More: What else can you make with orange rounds? What other fruity friends can you make?

4. Place a blueberry in the center of each orange round on your caterpillar's body, and add two more raisins at the bottom of each orange circle for legs.

Turn the page for a juicy treat!

Orange Blossom's Punch

This is a perfect party punch!

What You Need

- Flower ice cube tray
- ¼ cup cranberry juice
- ¼ cup orange juice
- Ginger ale
- Utensils: Spoon, glass, measuring cup, butter knife (optional)

Makes: 1 juicy serving

2. Remove the ice cube tray from the freezer. Bend the tray slightly to help the cubes pop out, or use a butter knife to loosen them.

3. Drop your fruit juice ice cubes into a glass. Then fill the glass with ginger ale. Berry refreshing!

1. Using a spoon, fill three of the flower molds in your ice cube tray with cranberry juice. Fill the other three flowers with orange juice. Place in the freezer for 1 to 2 hours until frozen.

Dip into a fun dip on the next page!

Tutti Frutti Orange Dip

This creamy fruit dip is berry yummy! Decorate the dip with some funny faces for some extra fun!

1. In a small bowl, add the sour cream, sugar, orange juice, and orange extract. Stir the ingredients together.

2. To make a sunny orange-colored dip, add 2 drops of red food coloring and 3 drops of yellow food coloring. Mix until the dip looks orange and creamy!

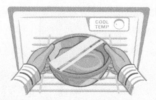

3. Cover the bowl with plastic wrap and refrigerate for about an hour.

What You Need

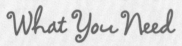

- 1 cup sour cream
- 1 ½ tablespoons sugar
- 1 tablespoon orange juice
- ¼ teaspoon orange extract
- Food coloring (red and yellow)
- Utensils: Measuring cups and spoons, small bowl, spoon, small serving bowl or fruit cups, plastic wrap

Serves: 8 sweet friends

4. Make some funny faces on your dip with fruit, if you like. Dip your favorite fruits into the dip, or add a dollop of dip to individual fruit cups!

Turn the page to see what Orange Blossom loves to take on picnics!

Friendship Fruit Salad

Orange Blossom shares this yummy fruit salad with her berry best friends!

What You Need

- Paper towels
- 2 navel oranges or mandarin oranges from a can
- 10 strawberries
- Optional: Apples, bananas, red and green grapes, pears, watermelon, and cantaloupe
- Utensils: Butter knife, cutting board, a serving dish or individual fruit cups

Serves: 8 friends

1. What kinds of fruits would you like to have in your friendship salad? Gather the fruits together, wash them in cold water, and dry them with paper towels.

2. Get your cutting board and butter knife ready. With an adult's help, remove the skin from the navel oranges and the stems from the strawberries.

3. Cut the oranges and strawberries into bite-size pieces. If you're using canned mandarin oranges, drain the juices and add the slices to your fruit salad.

5. Place the fruit salad into a pretty serving dish or into individual fruit cups for your friends.

4. Add your favorite fruits to the salad. Will you cut up an apple, peel and slice a banana, add whole grapes, or slice up a pear? It's up to you! Watermelon and cantaloupe might be yummy, too!

Here's More: You can serve your Friendship Fruit Salad with Tutti Frutti Orange Dip (see page 31) for a special treat!

Turn the page for a sweet icy treat!

33

Sunny Orange Slushy

*O*range Blossom and I like to eat this berry sweet icy treat any time of day!

What You Need

- ½ lemon
- 1 cup hot tap water
- ¼ cup sugar
- 2 cups orange juice
- Utensils: Measuring cups, small bowl, plastic container with lid, spoons, cups
- Optional: Hand-held juicer, plastic wrap

Serves: 4 berry cool friends

1. Have an adult cut a lemon in half. Juice half of the lemon with a spoon or with a hand-held juicer. Pour the juice into a small bowl.

2. Pour the hot tap water into a plastic container. Stir in the sugar until it dissolves.

3. Add in the lemon juice and the orange juice, and stir the ingredients together.

5. Remove your orange ice from the freezer. Spoon the slushy into cups and share with your berry cool friends!

4. Cover the plastic container with its lid or plastic wrap. Place it in the freezer. Freeze for about 4 to 6 hours, or until the mixture is slushy.

Here's More: You can serve your Sunny Orange Slushy with fresh orange slices for a berry sweet treat!

Turn the page for a creamy orange drink!

Fizzy Orange Float

Orange Blossom and I love to whip up this yummy dessert drink!

What You Need

- 6-ounce can of orange juice concentrate, partially thawed
- ½ cup milk
- 1 liter of berry cold ginger ale
- Orange sherbet
- Utensils: Measuring cups and spoons, pitcher, large spoon, tall float glasses
- Optional: Orange extract, food coloring (red and yellow), ice cream scoop, orange slice candy

Makes: 6 to 8 flavor-rific floats

1. Using a large spoon, combine the partially thawed orange juice concentrate, milk, and the ginger ale in a pitcher.

2. Stir in ¼ teaspoon of orange extract, if you like, to give your float a fun fizzy flavor.

3. Add food coloring, if you like, to make your float a sunny orange color. Mix in 4 drops of red food coloring and 6 drops of yellow food coloring.

4. Place one to two scoops of orange sherbet into each tall float glass. Pour in your orange fizzy drink and serve!

ORANGE SHERBET

Kitchen tip: If you run warm tap water over an ice cream scoop or large spoon, it makes it easier to dish out your frozen sherbet.

Here's More: You can decorate your float glasses with orange slice candy.

Orange Blossom's Answer Page

Butterfly Garden Hunt (pages 12–13)

Mix n' Match Fruit Game
(pages 22–23)

A. strawberry patch
B. watermelon vine
C. blueberry bush
D. orange tree
E. banana tree

5 Ways to Slice an Orange
(pages 26–27)

These pairs of groups add up to 10:

A and F $(7 + 3)$
B and G $(2 + 8)$
C and I $(9 + 1)$
D and H $(5 + 5)$
E and J $(6 + 4)$

Hint:
$1 + 9 = 10$
$2 + 8 = 10$
$3 + 7 = 10$
$4 + 6 = 10$
$5 + 5 = 10$

More Sweet Strawberryland Adventures COMING SOON!

To Our Berry Sweet Friend,

Thank you for sharing this fun and fruity orange adventure with us! <u>Orange</u> you glad you came along? We had a berry fun time with Orange Blossom's favorite fruit—the berry sweet orange—and her favorite fluttering friend Marmalade! Like an orange, you grow sweeter each day!

See you soon for our next Strawberryland adventure!

Your berry best friends,

Strawberry Shortcake,

ORANGE BLOSSOM,

and Marmalade

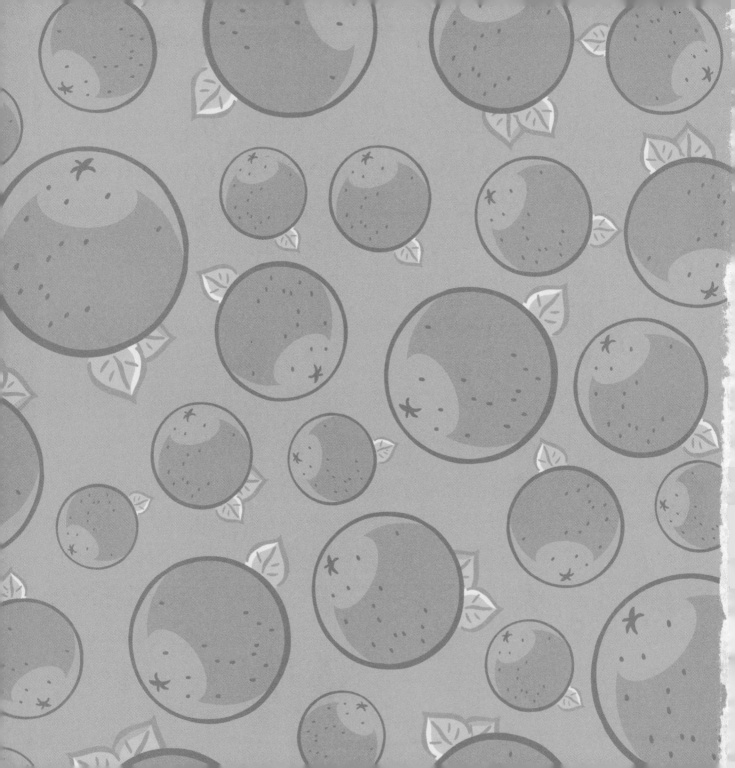